Dragon Booster™

OPPOSING FORCE

Adapted by James Gelsey
Based on an original script
written by Rob Travalino
Created by Kevin Mowrer
Rob Travalino

VOLO
an imprint of
HYPERION BOOKS FOR CHILDREN
New York

TM The Story Hat Properties, LLC, used under license by Alliance Atlantis.
© 2004 ApolloScreen GmbH and Co. Filmproduktion KG. © 2003 The Story Hat Properties, LLC. All Rights Reserved.
Alliance Atlantis with the stylized "A" design is a trademark of Alliance Atlantis Communications Inc.
The Story Hat Logo is a trademark of The Story Hat, LLC.

Volo® is a registered trademark of Disney Enterprises, Inc.
Volo/Hyperion Books for Children are imprints of
Disney Children's Book Group, L.L.C.

Printed in the United States of America

First Edition
1 3 5 7 9 10 8 6 4 2

This book is set in 13.5 New Aster.

ISBN 0-7868-3774-8

CHAPTER 1

It was a particularly gloomy afternoon in Mid City, the second highest of Dragon City's seven levels, and home to most of its inhabitants. People were scurrying about, doing their best to get errands done without getting soaked. A few customers dashed up the steps of the Dragon City Bank, hoping to make it inside before the bank closed for the day.

As passersby looked on, the elaborate stone archway over the bank's glass door began to vibrate. The door itself trembled as the rumbling grew louder. Then, without warning, the glass door shattered and exploded out toward the street as the bank's stone facade crumbled.

An enormous green Bull-class dragon burst forth. Screams from inside the bank filled the air. The massive beast paused ever so slightly so its rider could savor the horror of the moment. Then the dragon thundered down the stone steps, its purplish markings becoming something of a blur as it picked up speed.

Within seconds, six blue Dragon City security dragons raced past the bank, hoping to catch the elusive criminal. A rash of bank robberies had plagued Dragon City over the past few weeks. Each robbery had involved a green Bull-class dragon and a masked rider. This was clearly that duo. So far, no one had been able to catch the robber.

The Bull-class dragons were known for their extreme power, but speed was not among their attributes. But, somehow, whenever the Dragon City security officers cornered the culprit, he, with his dragon, managed to disappear.

The masked rider steered his dragon through the maze of Mid City streets and soon managed to shake off the security detail. As the pair rounded the next corner, the rider flipped up his mask and saw something that made him pull his Bull-class dragon to a screeching halt.

Before him, at a distance, was the

Dragon Booster. "You look kinda lost," he said with a smile. "Bank's the other way. What do you say you return that stuff before someone gets hurt?"

The Dragon Booster was sitting on Beau, the Black-and-Gold Dragon of Legend. Beau could be a ferocious and impressive sight, enough to scare almost anyone off. But instead of taking the Dragon Booster's advice, the rider smiled and gave his dragon a swift kick. The Bull-class dragon thundered down the street—straight toward Beau and the Dragon Booster. At the last possible moment, Beau leaped aside. The other dragon slammed into the side of a building with fierce impact.

"You know, we could keep this up all

day," said the Dragon Booster, "but if we do, your dragon's gonna have quite a headache."

Beau stalked menacingly toward the robber and his green dragon. As Beau came closer, the Dragon Booster noticed that the rider was wearing a Grip of the Dragon crew jacket. What he didn't notice was that the rider was smiling.

"We'll see who has the headache," the rider called out. He pushed his dragon forward and took off in the opposite direction. The dragon ran into the base of an enormous billboard pole. The force of the crash crumbled the base and slowly toppled the pole and billboard. It looked as if the sign were headed directly for a mother and her small child, who were crossing on the opposite side of the street. The green dragon raced off as Beau and the Dragon Booster sprang into action. The Dragon Booster couldn't let anything happen to innocent bystanders . . . not on his watch.

The Dragon Booster sprinted toward the helpless woman and her child. He raised his arms and braced himself for impact. The billboard fell squarely into the Dragon Booster's hands.

"You might want to move," the Dragon Booster grunted under the weight of the billboard. "This thing is kinda heavy."

The mother and daughter wasted no time in darting into the crowd that had begun to gather.

The Dragon Booster felt his arms begin to shake beneath the billboard.

"A little help here would be nice, Beau," he shouted.

Beau generated a mag-burst that lifted the Dragon Booster and the billboard about ten feet off the ground. Then he used the magnetic energy to yank his rider out from under the sign and safely down onto his back. The billboard slammed to the ground.

"Thanks, Beau," said the Dragon Booster. "Now, let's see if we can catch up with our friend."

Beau galloped off in the direction of the green Bull-class dragon. The Dragon Booster kept his eyes peeled and decided to check in with his best friend, Parmon Sean, for some guidance.

"What've you got, Parm?" asked the Dragon Booster.

"That was very impressive maneuvering, Artha," Parmon said. Parmon was one of the only people who knew the Dragon Booster's true identity: an ordinary teenager named Artha Penn. Parmon was standing on top of a nearby building keeping tabs on Artha and Beau . . . just as he always did. He peered through his high-tech binoculars as Artha's younger brother, Lance, surveyed the area with his naked eye.

"The perpetrator is escaping at a rather high rate of speed," Parmon reported.

"Tell me the way, Parm," Artha replied.

Parmon adjusted his binoculars to get a fix on the criminal.

"Go right . . . right!" he instructed. "Straight, Artha. Now go—aargh! I'm losing it!" The image in Parmon's binoculars blurred into several indistinguishable blobs. Parmon frantically rolled the control wheel back and forth, trying to restore the focus.

Lance noticed that Parmon was having some trouble, so he decided to get in on the action. "I'm going to cut them off,"

Lance announced. He flipped down his visor and took off on his dragon, Fracshun.

"Lance, where are you going?" Parmon called. He watched Fracshun gallop away, realizing that there was nothing he could do or say to stop Lance. With a sigh, Parmon returned to fixing his binocs.

"Hold on, Artha," Parmon said. "My color sensors need tweaking. They're supposed to modulate light-wave and radio-wave frequencies, but they seem to be malfunctioning!"

Down on the street, the Dragon Booster brought Beau to a stop. "What's malfunctioning is your directions, Parm," he said. "We'll never find him now."

Just then, Lance and Fracshun scurried

into an alley near the Dragon Booster. Looking around, Lance noticed the robber and the green dragon in the distance.

"He's right there!" Lance shouted into his comm link.

The sound of Lance's voice caught Artha off guard, and a pang of worry shot through his body. Ever since his father had disappeared, Artha had felt responsible for Lance's well-being. The last thing he wanted was for anything to happen to his little brother.

"Lance, what are you doing down here?" he asked.

"I can help!" Lance replied.

"Stay here with Parm, Lance," Artha instructed. "He needs you."

Without another look, Artha urged

Beau forward, and together they raced off after the robber. They followed the criminal through a series of alleys that dead-ended at a tangle of enormous metal ducts. The ducts provided ventilation for the lower levels of Dragon City. The Dragon Booster spied the green Bull-class dragon calmly standing in front of a tangle of ducts, chewing on what looked to be the remnants of a Draconee-Yum energy bar. The robber was not with him.

Artha surveyed the spaghetti bowl of duct work and shook his head. There was no way to know where the robber had gone.

"Scales!" Artha exclaimed. "I lost him!"

CHAPTER 2

The Dragon Booster glared at the impossible tangle of ventilation ducts. The robber he was chasing could have jumped down any one of them. As Artha's frustration at letting the criminal get away began to grow, Parmon's voice blasted through the comm link.

"I can see him! In the duct!" shouted Parmon.

"How?" asked the Dragon Booster.

Parmon—a real gearhead—was more

than happy to explain.

"Heat! It's just another wavelength my binocs can dial into," he said. "I can see his heat imprint right through the metal duct." From his perch on top of a neighboring building, Parmon was able to zero in on the robber's image crawling through the ventilation tubing.

Artha's frustration immediately switched to anticipation. He could still catch this guy!

"Well, which duct is it?" he asked

Parmon. He didn't want to waste time.

"The bottom one," came the reply through the comm link.

Jumping off Beau, the Dragon Booster found the lowest opening and dived into it headfirst. The shaft began a sharp descent and twisted its way through the hidden inner workings of Dragon City. He bounced his way down, his special armor pinging as it banged along the metallic tubing.

Using his binoculars, Parmon followed his friend's bumpy descent.

"Uh, Artha, I meant the other bottom one," he said.

"Thanks, Parm!" Artha replied, sounding more than a little annoyed.

The Dragon Booster landed with a

THUD. After taking a moment to clear his head, he began crawling along the duct works. He carefully slid down another slope in the tubing and came to a stop beside a discarded jacket. Upon closer inspection, the Dragon Booster discovered Grip of the Dragon crew insignia on the sleeve.

Hmmm, that's strange, he said to himself. Why would a Grip of the Dragon crew member throw away a perfectly good jacket?

The Dragon Booster carefully folded the jacket and managed to squeeze it beneath his armor. He heard some voices echoing in the distance and immediately began a speed-crawl through the duct to find the source. The voices grew louder and seemed to be coming from a ventilation grill on the duct's floor.

Carefully, he peered through the narrow openings. He was looking down on a massive round table. The murmuring voices became clearer as Artha began to put faces to them. Each voice belonged to a different Down City crew leader. They stood around the table, arguing with one another.

"Whoa!" Artha gasped. "Hey, Parm!"

"Yes, Artha?" replied his friend.

"Our little trail leads to the Down City Council round table," Artha whispered. "You may want to listen in on this."

A bald, muscled man with serious brown eyes, green coveralls, and no neck stepped to the table and slammed down a mighty hammer. The crashing blow shook the table and caught the attention of the other crew leaders in the room.

"Silence!" the man with the hammer ordered. "I've had enough of your petty bickering!"

The others fell silent and cast their eyes upon Phistus, leader of the Grip of the Dragon crew, and head of the Down City Council.

"It is our duty to ensure peace between the dragon crews or there would be city-wide chaos," Phistus said. Each word out of his mouth sounded as if it weighed a hundred pounds. "That is what the Down City Council does, what it has done for centuries. Have you all forgotten that?"

Phistus stared coldly at the each of the

council members. Many refused to make eye contact with him and shrank from his gaze. Others caught his glance and turned away, scowling. Only one of the council members stared back defiantly: the leader of the Dragon Eye crew, Moordryd Paynn.

Moordryd and his crew were notorious throughout Down City for their desire—and ability—to strike terror into the hearts of Dragon City citizens. It was Moordryd Paynn, in fact, who had started the series of events that caused Artha Penn to find his calling as the Dragon Booster.

Moordryd had once attempted to steal a black-and-gold dragon from Penn Stables—Beau. Connor Penn, Artha's father, had bred this dragon into existence, and Word Paynn, Moordryd's father, wanted him for his own evil purposes. As a result of Moordryd's stealing attempt, Penn Stables caught fire, Connor Penn disappeared, and Beau chose young Artha Penn as its rider. This last act fulfilled an ancient prophecy, bringing together the Black-and-Gold Dragon of Legend and his Dragon Booster. Together, they were supposed to prevent the world from slipping into another devastating dragon-human war.

Right now, Moordryd Paynn was more interested in challenging Phistus.

"The problem isn't each other," Moordryd declared. "It's this so-called hero, the Dragon Booster."

Murmurs of agreement buzzed around the table.

"I hear that one has nothing to fear from him," Phistus replied. "Unless, of course, you are a thief!"

The murmurs grew into grumbling as the other council members began to smell trouble brewing between Phistus and Moordryd.

One of the council members stood.

"We all just have to do what we can to get out of Squire's End and have a chance to race the Elite Class," he said, trying to defuse the growing tension.

"I admit that we all have dreams of greater things," Phistus said. Then he turned and glared at Moordryd. "It's just that some of our methods are honorable, and some are questionable."

"We're all the same, Phistus," Moordryd replied. "Down City crews . . . all the same."

Phistus exploded in anger. "Not me!"

The two adversaries locked stares without moving. Sirens began to blare in the distance, and some of the council members eyed one another nervously. A door flew open, and a Dragon Eye crew member entered the room, making a beeline for Moordryd. He whispered something to Moordryd, who nodded solemnly.

From his hiding spot, the Dragon Booster leaned forward for a better view of the crew member talking to Moordryd. Something about him looked familiar.

"I know that face," Artha said to himself. "But how?"

A series of images from the day's events flashed across his mind. Then he had it: the crew member speaking to Moordryd was the same person who had robbed the bank and toppled the billboard.

So Moordryd Paynn had something to do with this, Artha said to himself. Why am I not surprised?

CHAPTER 3

The tension in the Down City Council chamber was extreme. Phistus was not shy about expressing his disdain for Moordryd Paynn. And Moordryd had no problem thumbing his nose at Phistus's authority. The other council members could only wait and hope that something would keep the two opposing forces apart. After his crew member had finished delivering some news, Moordryd turned and faced the council.

"It seems we have a little problem," he began. "You see, my friend here just spent the last twenty minutes hiding in a ditch to stay away from an army of Dragon City security. And from the Dragon Booster."

"A ditch?" Artha chuckled from his secret hiding spot in the ventilation shaft above the chamber. "Oh, boy, Moordryd, you gotta work on your lies."

"And your point is?" Phistus asked impatiently.

A thin smile crept across Moordryd's face. This was the part he was waiting for.

"Security followed *your* crew down from a little heist!" Moordryd declared.

"My crew? That's a lie!" Phistus shouted. His eyes narrowed as he glared across the table at Moordryd.

Moordryd reached into his jacket and took out a handheld radio transmitter. He flicked it on and turned up the volume, and a tinny voice filled the chamber.

"Eyewitnesses say that the bank robber was clearly identified as a Grip of the Dragon crew member," the announcer reported. *"Security is still searching for a green Bull-class dragon last seen—"*

Moordryd turned off the radio and stared at Phistus. All eyes around the council table also turned to Phistus.

"Lies!" Phistus roared.

"Look whose foot is in his mouth now," Moordryd replied.

Phistus gazed around the room and felt the heat of everyone's stare burning him. He rose from the table and took a step back. His muscles tensed, and he reached down for his mighty hammer. Phistus grasped the powerful weapon and raised it over his head. Then, with all his might, he smashed it down on the table, shattering the once-solid piece of furniture.

The other council members jumped back, except for Moordryd, who calmly grabbed the black control rope from beneath his cape and whipped it into the air with a mighty *crack!* Phistus and

Moordryd were locked in an intense stare-down.

"You have disgraced the council," Moordryd accused. "And, upon my ancient rights, and by Dragon Joust, I challenge your leadership!"

The council members began shouting at Phistus, Moordryd, and one another. The whole chamber erupted into chaos and became a free-for-all. For the first time that afternoon, the Dragon Booster actually felt a little nervous.

"This is bad . . . very bad," he said quietly to Parmon through the comm link. "If Moordryd takes over the council, Dragon City will fall into chaos."

Before Parmon could answer, Artha moved away from the vent so that he could get back to the surface. As he did, his foot pressed against a rusty metal pipe that gave way with a ferocious clang. Moordryd looked up. "What was that?" he said.

Artha felt the metal duct beneath his body begin to move. In an instant, the whole ventilation shaft cracked open and dumped him onto the floor in the middle of the council chamber.

"A spy!" cried out one of the council members.

"Nice place you've got here," Artha said boldly. He stood up. "Sorry about the mess."

"It's the Dragon Booster!" Moordryd shouted. "Get him!"

The Dragon Booster braced himself as

the council members circled around him. Moordryd Paynn stepped forward and cracked his black control whip.

"Nowhere to run, Dragon Booster," Moordryd said. "And nowhere to hide. Let's see you 'boost' your way out of this!"

Just as Moordryd took a step, the ground began to tremble. The council members looked around nervously, but the Dragon Booster just smiled. The trembling grew heavier until a deafening crash overwhelmed the chamber. When the dust cleared, the Black-and-Gold Dragon of Legend stood in the middle of a pile of rubble that just moments earlier had been a stone wall. Everyone in the chamber froze as Beau glared at them.

"You may wanna back off . . . quickly,"

the Dragon Booster said. "He doesn't like crowds."

The council members were more than happy to oblige; they gave Beau and the Dragon Booster plenty of space. Artha sauntered over to Beau and patted him on the head. Beau lowered his head and placed his nose beneath the Dragon Booster's foot. With a quick snap, he flipped the Dragon Booster into the air, where he somersaulted, landing squarely in the saddle.

Beau roared ferociously, nearly blowing everyone over, and then spun around, exploding back through the opening in the wall.

The council members crowded around the hole, staring after the Dragon Booster in awe. Once again, the pair had gotten away . . . and no one knew who they were. Only Moordryd and Phistus remained unmoved by the action.

"This isn't over, Phistus," Moordryd warned. "I'll see you at the joust!"

CHAPTER 4

Artha Penn narrowly evaded the swinging mace ball hurtling directly toward his head. It was one of many similar devices in an endless gauntlet of sorts that was part of a vigorous training program created by Mortis. The training was meant to help Artha develop the necessary skills to fulfill his destiny as the Dragon Booster.

Mortis was the mysterious Dragon Priest who had been advising Artha ever since Beau had chosen him as the Dragon

Booster. Artha and Beau, usually with Lance and Parmon at their sides, visited Mortis regularly in the abandoned dragon temples of Old City, which was the bottommost level of Dragon City and —except for Mortis—completely deserted.

Artha tried to balance his long staff in his hand while dodging the relentless barrage of attacks. Most of the devices consisted of nothing more than mechanical arms mounted on tall metal pylons. The height of the arms varied, making it difficult for Artha to know where he would get hit. As the arms swung around and around, Artha and Beau had to avoid contact with them, or be knocked to the ground. Sometimes Artha ducked down. Sometimes Beau jumped. Sometimes

Artha jumped and Beau ducked. Sometimes Artha swatted away the oncoming attack with his staff. Fortunately, Artha and Beau managed to maneuver their way through the course with continuing success . . . and few injuries.

While Artha worked on honing his skills, Mortis watched in silence. Parmon Sean kept an eye on Artha's technique. He made mental notes, intending to share his suggestions and comments afterward. Lance also kept himself busy. The ten-year-old played with his remote-controlled dragon. Each time he saw Artha do something on the training course, Lance imitated the moves with his toy dragon.

After the eighth run, Beau trudged off

the training course and walked over to the others. Parmon noticed that as they got closer, Artha and Beau were breathing heavily.

"How was that?" Artha asked.

"Better, but the machines are only set to challenge-level two," Mortis answered.

Artha couldn't believe his ears. Level two? It felt more like level twenty-two to him. But Artha didn't dare say that aloud. He knew better than to question Mortis and his methods, so he kept his mouth shut. Parmon, on other hand, didn't always exercise the same mouth-shutting restraint.

"I can't believe that Moordryd challenged Phistus to joust," he said. "Everyone knows Phistus is the best jouster in Dragon City."

"Moordryd is obviously planning to cheat," Artha spat out. "And I'll bet his father, Word, is in on it, too!"

Mortis nodded slightly, indicating his agreement. "If Moordryd beats Phistus and becomes the council leader, many powerful crews will be lured to Word Paynn and his false promises," Mortis said solemnly. "He would then use these lost souls for his own purposes."

Artha immediately knew what purposes Mortis was talking about.

"A dragon-human war," he said.

Artha had learned about Word's plans for a dragon-human war the first time he had met Mortis. That was also right after Moordryd Paynn had tried to steal Beau and started the fire that had destroyed most of Penn Stables and cost Artha and Lance their father. It was not a pleasant memory.

On that day, Artha discovered that Word Paynn was behind the attempted dragon-napping. He and his son had their hearts set on stealing the legendary dragon. Artha had since learned that Word would stop at nothing to get his hands on Beau and use the dragon's power to start the war to end all wars. It was the Dragon Booster's job to keep that from happening. No matter what the cost.

Inside Word Paynn's command center, a wall of plasma monitors replayed a scene familiar to the two people watching. Word and Moordryd watched the chaos that had ripped apart the Down City Council chambers earlier that afternoon. Without taking his eyes from the monitors, Word addressed his son.

"Congratulations, Moordryd," Word said. "The fool Phistus is now ready to fall! You see, my plan worked flawlessly."

Moordryd welcomed the opportunity to help his father bring about instability and terror. But he hated the suggestion that it was Word's idea alone—and not Moordryd's own hard work—that had brought about the intended results. Nevertheless, Moordryd focused on the future . . . and tried not to upset his father.

"I'm interested in the rest of your plan," Moordryd said. "Where is this so-called

Wraith Dragon of yours?"

Word smiled ever so slightly as he touched his fingertip to his headpiece. A pair of special yellow lenses emerged and covered his eyes. Word picked up a small remote-control unit and turned to face Moordryd. He pressed two buttons on the unit and waited.

Moordryd watched his father with a puzzled look. Had he missed something? An instant later, he felt something tug at

the back of his collar. A powerful force began lifting him off the ground. Moordryd tried to turn but couldn't see anything except his father. The higher Moordryd got, the more panic he felt. This panic was nothing compared to the hot, steamy sensation that pulsed down his neck.

"Let me down!" Moordryd cried, kicking at the unseen attacker. "Let me down!"

Word savored the moment and then placed his thumb over another button on the remote-control device.

"Of course," he said with a smile. Then he pressed the button.

Moordryd dropped to the floor like a stone. He rubbed the back of his neck as Word pushed something else on the remote-control device. As if by magic, a dark purple dragon began to appear in the space behind Moordryd. Moordryd spun around and came face to face with the dragon. Strange black control gear cloaked the dragon's head and much of its body. The dragon stepped forward, and Moordryd recognized the warm, damp breath that had freaked him out just moments earlier.

"The Wraith Dragon is simply a function of my black-draconium mind-control and invisibility gear," Word said. He handed the remote-control device to Moordryd, who fumbled with it. To Word, the dragon was a toy. Another way to start his war. With a twitch of his fingers he could make the dragon become invisible. It was a trick that would come in handy soon.

"Be thankful it shall be fighting on your side," Word added. "Now, go! Defeat Phistus, and deliver control of the Down City Council to me!"

Word turned and left his son and the dragon alone in the command center. Moordryd pressed a button on the device and watched the dragon fade into nothingness. As he mastered the remote-control device, his confidence returned.

"All right, Phistus," Moordryd declared. "Let's get ready to rumble!"

CHAPTER 5

Once again, Artha and Beau were smashing their way through the ramming pylons that came quickly out of the wall. Lance was imitating his brother's moves, but with a twist. He had attached a tiny jousting stick to his toy dragon, and was directing the dragon toward three rows of little dragon racers that he had arranged.

"Remote-control jousting is drac!" Lance cheered. "Bang! Boom! You're not so big! Pow!"

The remote-control dragon crashed through the crowd of toys, spilling little dragon racers across the floor. The dragon scurried around Lance's legs before veering out of control; it raced over Parmon's foot. Lance laughed.

"Ouch!" Parmon cried. "Lance! Be careful!"

"But I wanna help!" Lance replied.

"Help what? Break my toes?" Parmon asked.

Even though Lance was laughing, deep down he felt a little frustrated. Lance was proud of Artha and thought it was cool that his brother was the Dragon Booster. But he also wished he could do more than just play with his toy dragon. He wanted to get into the action.

He watched as Artha and Beau once again trudged off to start on the training course. They were breathing more heavily than ever.

"No more today, Mortis," Artha gasped. "We're totally exhausted." Beau grunted in agreement and vented some steam through his skin. Artha lay forward against the back of Beau's neck.

"Dragon Booster!" Mortis thundered. His booming voice echoed throughout the dragon temple—and Artha's head. Artha and Beau snapped to attention.

"You have tasks ahead that require endurance, willpower, and an inner strength you never knew you had," Mortis said, his voice measured and encouraging. Artha, Beau, Parmon, and even Lance hung on his every word.

"If there is one lesson you must learn, it is to know the true meaning of *heart*," Mortis continued. "And never to give up!"

The meaning of Mortis's words sank in. Artha nodded, and Beau took a deep breath.

"C'mon, Beau, let's go!" Artha said, rallying his strength. Beau spun around and charged back through the challenge course. "This time, level three!"

Mortis nodded approvingly. Out of the corner of his eye, he noticed Lance sadly walking away, his toy dragon clutched tightly in his arms. Mortis turned and followed him.

"What troubles you, Lance?" he asked.

Lance stopped and looked up, surprised

that Mortis was actually speaking to him. Once the moment of shock passed, Lance furrowed his brow once more.

Mortis seemed to know what was on the youngster's mind. "Your day will come," he said. "You just have to be patient."

"Everybody's always telling me I'm not big enough for this, and I'm too small for that!" Lance whined. "It scrapes my scales!"

Deep down, Mortis admired Lance's spirit and could understand his frustration.

"They're just trying to protect you," Mortis said. "Remember, it's not how big you are, Lance Penn, it's the size of your heart that matters. And when I look at you,

I see a heart as big as a mountain."

Mortis gave Lance a reassuring pat on the shoulder. Lance smiled up at Mortis, happy . . . for the moment.

After another grueling hour of training, Artha and Beau were completely wiped out. Beau lay on his side and rested. Artha leaned up against his dragon friend, his mind lost in thought. Nearby, Parmon and Lance sat quietly while Mortis stood over them. A thought hit Artha, and he looked over at Mortis.

"If Moordryd actually does beat Phistus, does he automatically get to control the Down City Council?" he asked.

"Yes." Mortis nodded. Then he added, "But the ancient rules dictate that he may be challenged by one other on that day to prove his worthiness."

"Anyone would be better than Moordryd," Artha said. As the words left Artha's mouth, Parmon noticed a sudden flicker of light in his eyes. Parmon knew his friend very well, and that flicker made it very clear that Artha was planning something.

"Come on, Beau," Artha said, jumping up. "Level three, one more time." Beau looked up at Artha and knew exactly what he was thinking. They had to face Moordryd—and they needed to be ready. Beau wasted no time in joining the Dragon Booster back on the challenge course.

"What? Are you two serious?" Parmon asked. "I can't think of anyone who'd be foolish enough to go up against the guy who had just beaten Phistus."

Artha climbed on top of Beau and smiled down at Parmon.

"Anyone?" he asked teasingly, before crashing through the course once again.

CHAPTER 6

"Dragon-racing crews of Squire's End! The main event is about to begin!"

Race Marshall Budge soared above the crowd on his judging platform as the crowd below roared in anticipation of the evening's excitement. Budge, a rotund little man, served as the official judge for all Down City dragon races. On this night, however, his job was to referee the Joust of the Century between Phistus and Moordryd Paynn.

The jousting arena was actually part of the larger Squire's End dragon racetrack. The straightaway that served as the track's starting point was the perfect length for a jousting competition. The stands lined both sides of the track and were packed with Dragon City residents who wanted to see if anyone could defeat Phistus, the reigning jousting champion. In the very center of the stands, about halfway up, a private viewing box remained empty. But not for long.

"Well, it seems we have a special guest for tonight's event," Race Marshall Budge announced. "Welcome, Mr. Paynn, sir."

A hush fell over the stadium as all eyes turned to Word Paynn, who had entered the private box. Word nodded in Race

Marshall Budge's direction and then took his seat. As he sat down, a slow hum filled the stands and gradually changed to a full roar as the fans got back into the spirit of the night.

"First, the challenger," Race Marshall Budge announced. "You know him from street racing and as leader of the Dragon Eye crew: Moordryd Paaaaaaaaynn!"

Moordryd rode out from the opening

beneath the center of the stands. He wore his standard black-and-purple racing uniform and sat on his dragon, Decepshun. Moordryd looked up at the crowd and was greeted by boos, groans, and the occasional cheer.

"Let's see what kind of reception they give me after this joust," Moordryd whispered bitterly. "They'll be cheering then."

"And now, spanning a decade of battle competition," Budge began, "he's the Grip of the Dragon leader, head of the Down City Council, and all-time Dragon City jousting champion: Phiiiiiiisssssstuuuuuuussss!"

Phistus rode out to cheering and applause with a couple of boos thrown in. His dark green Bull-class dragon grunted at Decepshun. After a few moments, Race

Marshall Budge managed to quiet the crowd.

"It's the best two out of three rounds," he announced. "Rules are simple. When you hit the ground, you lose the round. Combatants, take your places."

Phistus and Moordryd rode their dragons to opposite ends of the jousting track. Each dragon was outfitted with a full complement of green ramming armor. Both riders carried long jousting poles. Upon reaching the starting lines, the dragons turned around. Moordryd and Phistus glared at each other from across the track. Moordryd glanced over his left shoulder and noticed a hunched figure standing in the shadows.

It was Cain, Moordryd's second in

command in the Dragon Eye crew. Cain wore special yellow lenses and held a remote-control device in his hands. Cain and Moordryd made eye contact. Cain smiled and gave Moordryd a thumbs-up. Taking a deep breath, Moordryd turned and once again stared at Phistus.

Race Marshall Budge picked up a small golden gong. He struck the instrument with a tiny mallet, and an enormous sound echoed along the track.

Phistus and Moordryd sprang forward on their dragons. Their jousting sticks drawn, the riders urged their dragons on and picked up speed. Off to the side, Cain pressed a series of buttons on the remote-control device. The Wraith Dragon quietly galloped up alongside Phistus, but Phistus couldn't see it because of its invisibility gear. The Wraith Dragon slammed its body against Phistus's dragon, knocking the massive green creature off its stride. The sudden impact took Phistus by surprise. He looked to his side, expecting to see another dragon. But there was nothing. Phistus's brief moment of utter confusion was all Moordryd needed. As Phistus faced forward, Moordryd delivered a powerful blast with his jousting pole and knocked Phistus clean off his dragon. Phistus crashed to the ground as his dragon raced on. The audience roared in a mixture of surprise and delight at what they had just witnessed.

"Owww! That's gotta hurt," Race Marshall Budge announced from his floating platform above the track. "So the first of three rounds goes to . . . Moordryd Paynn. Jousters, prepare for round two!"

Phistus shook off the effects of the blow and stood up. His dragon returned to him, and Phistus got on. They rode back to their starting position at the far end of the track, Phistus's rock-solid resolve a bit shaken by the mysterious jolt he had received. But his anger at Moordryd more than compensated for the tiny loss in his concentration. Phistus was determined not to let Moordryd get the best of him again.

Race Marshall Budge struck the gong once more. The dragons lurched forward, and the scene played out almost exactly as it had before. Cain worked the controls and brought the Wraith Dragon within striking distance. The invisible creature once again slammed into Phistus and his dragon, this time knocking Phistus's jousting pole to the ground. The momentary loss of balance unnerved Phistus, but he recovered—barely. As he reached for another weapon, Moordryd once again delivered a powerful blow that sent him tumbling along the track. The crowd went wild.

"Incredible! Phistus has been defeated!" Budge shouted, getting caught up in the excitement of the moment. "I give you the jousting champion of Dragon City and, according to the ancient laws, the new leader of the Down City Council: Moordryd Paynn!"

Moordryd pumped his fists in the air.